Paddy the Penguin

Paddy
the Penguin

by Paul Galdone

Thomas Y. Crowell Company New York

1 2 3 4 5 6 7 8 9 10

Paddy Penguin watched the gulls fly high above him. As he watched he wished that he, too, could dip and soar over the frosty snow and sparkling ice. But penguins are birds that cannot fly. Their wings are only flippers. And flippers are meant for paddling and swimming, not for flying.

It was a bright morning in the Antarctic, very near the South Pole. Paddy had just finished his breakfast of fish, and his friends were waddling over to play with him.

Every day after breakfast, Paddy and his friends played games. Their favorite game was King of the Mountain. Paddy scrambled up to the top of a mound of snow. Another penguin quickly followed him and pushed Paddy off the top. The game had begun.

Everyone tried to get to the top of the snow mound, for the penguin who could stay there the longest would be the King of the Mountain.

What fun! More penguins tumbled down the slope and started to chase Paddy. He waddled as fast as he could across the ice.

All the other penguins followed him in single
file. The game had turned into Follow the Leader.
Paddy proudly led his friends across the snow
fields to their ice playground by the open sea.

Here they could dive as straight as a gull and could swim under water faster than most fish.

The next game they played was the High-Jump Game. This was a contest to see who could jump over the widest cracks in the ice. Paddy was a good jumper, but some of his friends were even better. They jumped so high and so far that it seemed as though they were flying. How Paddy wished *he* could fly.

Just as Paddy was about to take his turn in the jumping game, he saw a gull soar into the air. Still watching the gull, he jumped as high as he could and landed—plop—right on his clean white vest.

Enough of this, he said to himself. He whirled
on his belly and skimmed away over the glittering
ice. His feet moved as fast as the propeller of a
motor boat. This must be almost as fast as flying,
he thought. He waited for his friends to join him
and away they went to play Slide on Your Belly.

They all slid along rapidly, over glittering ice
and shiny snow. Then they came to the ocean.

But this did not stop their fun. They hopped on a
large cake of floating ice and off they went for a
ride. Waves pushed them along the icy shore.

All at once Paddy heard a strange whirring sound. He saw a huge gull flying above him toward the distant snowy peaks. It was the largest gull he had ever seen.

And this one had no wings!

Paddy waved and waved his flippers, but the bird roared noisily on and flew toward the white peaks.

A bird with no wings that can fly!
If he can do it, why can't I?

He left his friends and splashed ashore. He was going to find the strange bird.

He waddled and waddled and slid on his belly.

He jumped and he swam and he walked just about as far as a little penguin could.

He was getting very tired.

At last he saw the strange bird. There it sat, resting on a large sheet of ice. It was the biggest bird Paddy had ever seen.

And next to the strange bird stood the biggest penguin Paddy had ever seen.

The giant penguin waved his flipper toward Paddy. Paddy waved back.

Then Paddy waddled down to him and bowed
in a most polite manner.

The giant penguin bowed, too.

After they had looked at each other for a while, Paddy waddled slowly around the strange bird.

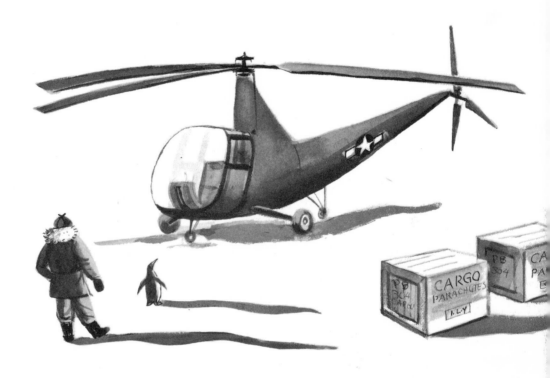

It never moved. Then the giant penguin fastened some funny strings under Paddy's flippers. He seemed to guess that Paddy wanted to fly. He lifted Paddy up and put him right inside the strange bird! Then the giant penguin climbed in after him. With a loud whirring noise the strange bird rose into the air.

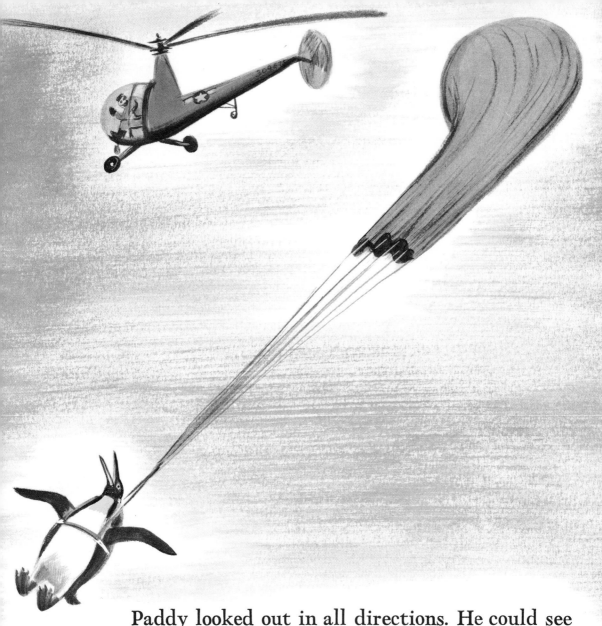

Paddy looked out in all directions. He could see high mountain peaks all around him. Far below he could see the water.

Then the giant penguin pushed Paddy gently out of the strange bird, right into the air.

Paddy felt a strong pull as the funny strings under his flippers tightened.

PADDY WAS FLYING!

He looked down and saw his papa and his
mama and all the friends he played games with.
The penguins waved and cheered.

Paddy landed with a bump.

His papa and mama rushed over and hugged him. Paddy's wish had come true. He had flown as high as any bird.

Now all his friends wanted to fly. Next day, after much waving and flipper flapping, Paddy led his friends to the place where the big bird stayed.

Single file the penguins started off behind
Paddy. They slid on their bellies and jumped over
cracks in the ice and slid on their bellies some more.

At last they came to the strange bird. Near it the giant penguin awaited them with surprise.

Paddy bowed proudly. The other penguins bowed, too. The giant penguin bowed back.

Paddy pointed his flipper toward the strange bird and waddled over to it. All the penguins followed him, this time in a double line.

The giant penguin fastened strings under each of the penguin's flippers and tucked them all one by one into the bird with no wings.

U! S 1077026

With a whir and a roar they were all soon up in the air.

The penguins shoved, chattered, and bumped each other. Each tried to get the best view. How high above the earth they were! How far below was the water!

And then Paddy waved his flipper toward the distant snowfield where their papas and mamas were waiting for them.

When they were right over them, the giant
penguin gently pushed them out of the strange
bird, one at a time.

The sky was filled with flying penguins!

One after another the penguins landed and fell into the flippers of their happy parents.

They all had flown at last!

Paddy and his friends shook off the funny strings, smoothed their vests, fell into line, and marched off for a game of King of the Mountain before supper.

It was so good to be home again.